FOLLOW THAT SLEIGH!
THE REINDEER WHO SAVED CHRISTMAS

Published by Scopus Films (London) Ltd.
30 Cliff Road, London NW1 9AG
15 Efratah Street, Jerusalem 93384

U.S.A. – Shapolsky Publishers Inc., 136 West 22nd Street, New York, NY 10011.

Printed and bound by Keterpress Enterprises, Jerusalem, Israel.
Color separations: Gamma Scan

10 9 8 7 6 5 4 3 2 1

ISBN: 0-944007-51-1

FOLLOW THAT SLEIGH!
THE REINDEER WHO SAVED CHRISTMAS

Story & Design by Dick Codor
Written by Michael Teitelbaum

Created in clay by Rony Oren

Photographs: Liora Codor

It was Christmas Eve...

Jennifer and Kevin were fast asleep. They dreamed of roasted chestnuts, fluffy snowdrifts and enormous giftboxes wrapped in red and green paper.

They had just begun dreaming about thick bars of chocolate when...

CRASH! CLUMP! CRASH!!!

The entire house shook. Something had landed on the roof.

Kevin sat up in bed.

"It's him, Jenny! He's here!"

Jennifer rubbed her eyes and said, "Wha-huh — smiddlenightssshhhh."

"I just know," said Kevin, "that he's brought me an awesome skateboard and a radio controlled Formula One race car and..."

"Kevin!" Jennifer was wide awake by now. "Out the window! Look!"

There under a silver moon, Santa's sleigh and reindeer glistened against the soft, white snow.

"Let's sneak downstairs!" said Kevin. "That way we'll see Santa."

CREAK CREAK CREAK! Down they crept. They hid behind the couch. When Kevin saw Santa's boots, he couldn't keep quiet. "It's him! It's Santa! He's bringing my —"

"Quiet, Kevin!" whispered Jennifer. "He'll hear you!"

Santa used his computer-watch to check with Elf Control, his hi-tech home base at the North Pole. Had these children been good this year?

Kevin looked at Santa's bag more closely. "Hey, it's empty. I don't think he brought me anything!"

"Always thinking about presents," scolded Jennifer. "Anyway, I'm sure he brought you something."

Just then, the green light flashed on Santa's watch. He reached into his empty-looking bag. From out of nowhere a pile of presents spilled onto the carpet.

"There! I can see the presemphghh..." shouted Kevin through the hand which Jennifer placed over his mouth.

Santa stoked the fire, settled himself comfortably in the armchair, and set his computer-watch for a five minute snooze. Soon his snores filled the room.

Kevin crept over to Santa's sack and peered into it.

"Where do all the presents come from?" he wondered. "Maybe there's more inside for me?"

Just then...

"Santa Claus is coming to town... DO-WA, DO-WA, DO-WA, DO-WAA..." came the sound of singing from outside.

"Listen, Kevin!" said Jennifer. "It's Santa's reindeer. They're singing! For us!"

Santa's magic bag was still in Kevin's hand when he and his sister rushed outside.

The reindeer smiled at them, threw back their antlers, and hit a perfect middle C.

"**W**ow!" exclaimed Kevin. "Look at this sleigh! It's about the coolest thing I've ever seen."

"Now Kevin," began Jennifer. "Don't get any of your ideas!"

"I just want to look around inside," said Kevin. "Come on. No one'll know."

"Kevin, this is not our property," said Jennifer. "Besides, what will Santa think?"

"Oh, don't be such a baby. Anyway, he'll never know," said Kevin. "He's fast asleep."

Kevin hopped into the sleigh and began to play with the buttons and knobs. "I wonder what this does," he thought. CLICK went the switch, WHIRR-WHIRR-WHIRR went the sleigh.

"DUM DUM DO WAA," sang the reindeer.

Jennifer climbed in cautiously.

"Come on, Kevin, the game's over, let's go back insi—" WHOOOSH!

"YAAAAA!!!" Jennifer screamed as the sleigh zoomed up into the sky with the reindeer, still singing, in the lead, and Kevin shouting with glee.

"Kevin, you bring this thing home right now!" yelled Jennifer.

Kevin turned dials and pulled levers, but he had no idea how the sleigh worked.

CHUGGA-CHUGGA went the sleigh. "Pilot to co-pilot! Come in please. Yahoo, this is much more fun than a skateboard!" roared Kevin.

BEE – EE – EP went Santa's watch. He awoke with a start, felt for his bag, and ran outside.

"Rollicking reindeers! What's going on!" exclaimed the jolly old fellow, who was not feeling very jolly at that moment. "What are those little rascals doing with my sleigh?"

TWEEP-TWEEP-TWEEP went the telephone on top of the radar screen at Elf Control. Mama Claus answered the call.

"Calm down, dear," she said. "Just tell Mama what's wrong."

"It's terrible!" cried Santa. "Just terrible! They've taken my sleigh! And my sack! You'd better send a rescue team right away, Mama, or I won't be able to deliver the presents by Christmas Day!"

"But Santa!" chirped one of the elves. "All the regular back-up sleighs are in the repair shop, and all of the reindeer are with your sleigh!"

Mama Claus scratched her head thoughtfully while the other elves looked at each other in silence.

Finally, one of them spoke up.

"But what about that reindeer who hangs out in the music department?" he said.

Everyone knew who he meant. Over the telephone they could hear Santa sigh.

Elvis, the rockin' reindeer, had always been, well, different from the others.

"Elvis!" Santa would call. SNAP, SNAP, SNAP went Elvis' hooves as he bopped to the tunes on his personal stereo. He was not a bad reindeer, he was just "too cool for words."

But right now, he was Santa's only hope.

Elvis' best friend was Nellie the Elf. "I know you're special," she always said. "You've got a real — Elvis, take those headphones off for a second — special sense about things. It will come in handy some day."

That day had arrived. Nellie hitched him up to her sleigh. "Santa's in trouble! Let's go!"

WHOOSH went the sleigh, as Elvis, with headphones on and hooves snapping, leaped into the air, and the two friends set off to save Santa, the kids and Christmas itself.

On a dark, deserted road three sad-looking men from *Three Kings Meals on Wheels* charity sat next to their broken truck.

"We'll never get these hot Christmas dinners to the homeless," moaned the first.

"How can we deliver meals on wheels when we don't have any wheels?" asked the second.

"Well, what shall we do?" said the third. "Wait for help to drop out of the sky?"

WUMP went the sleigh as it dropped out of the sky.

"Excuse us," said Jennifer. "You looked like you could use some help."

"Why did we have to land?" grumbled Kevin. "It's fun up there. I was just beginning to get the hang of it."

"Oh, come on Kevin." Jennifer gave him a look and turned back to the three miserable kings. "We're here to help. What can we do for you?"

"Nice sleigh!" said one of the kings, forgetting his troubles for the moment. "Where'd you get it?"

"It's ours," Kevin fibbed.

"Don't lie, Kevin," sighed Jennifer. "You know it's Santa's."

"Santa's, huh?" The second king thought for a moment. "Well, how about hitching up Santa's fancy sleigh to our truck? That way you could tow us into town."

"Do we have to?" asked Kevin.

But Jennifer had already decided. "Don't pay any attention to him, he's always like that. Now then — let's get those meals into town!"

CRUNCH, CRUNCH, CRUNCH went the snow as Santa paced nervously.

"Where on earth is my rescue team?" he fretted out loud. "If I don't catch up with my sleigh soon, children all over the world won't be getting their Christmas presents this year!"

"Yo, Santa!" came a voice from the North. "We're here!" Nellie and Elvis had come to the rescue.

"Elvis' sense of direction guided me through the night," said Nellie as Santa climbed aboard.

"Now then," said Santa, "let's get a move on!" He radioed Elf Control, "Mama, where are those kids?"

"Well, let me see," Mama began.

"Hurry, Mama, hurry!" pleaded Santa.

"Oh, here they are, I see them, right here on our radar screen," Mama called. "Forty miles North by Northwest. Off you go, dear!"

"With only one reindeer, it's going to be tough catching up," said Santa. "Now, Elvis, follow that sleigh!"

"Don't worry Santa," Nellie cried. "Elvis won't let you down! Will you Elvis? Elvis? ELVIS! FOLLOW THAT SLEIGH!"

MUNCH, MUNCH, MUNCH went the mouths of the happy people eating their hot Christmas dinners thanks to Kevin and Jennifer.

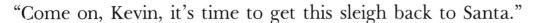

"Thank you," said the kings. "Without you and your snazzy sleigh, many people would have gone hungry this Christmas."

"Gosh," said Kevin. " I didn't know there were so many hungry people in the world."

"Come on, Kevin, it's time to get this sleigh back to Santa."

"Goodbye!" the children called, and ZOOM the sleigh took off into the night sky.

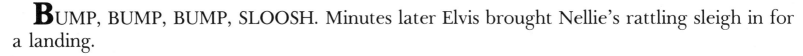

BUMP, BUMP, BUMP, SLOOSH. Minutes later Elvis brought Nellie's rattling sleigh in for a landing.

"We're looking for two children," Santa explained frantically. "One's about this tall, one's about this short. And, oh yes, they were in MY sleigh, pulled by MY reindeer."

"This tall? This short? Sleigh? Reindeer?" the kings repeated.

"That's right!"

"You just missed them!"

"Oh, fiddleferns!" exclaimed Santa. "Come on Nellie, we've got to keep after them!"

SWISH went the huge Christmas tree, swaying one way. SWOOSH as it swayed back the other way. A group of villagers were struggling to put up their tree. Jennifer wanted to help.

"Not again," protested Kevin, "there are still some knobs I haven't tried."

"Oh Kevin, stop thinking about yourself! Just swing the sleigh down over the tree."

So Kevin descended, but the sleigh began spinning. "Hey, we're upside down!"

"I know that, dummy! Just keep it steady," called Jennifer. "There, I've got the tree-top."

Down below, the villagers tied the tree securely while Jennifer held it from above.

THUMP. Kevin landed the sleigh.

"We'll never get the tree decorated in time," said one of the children.

"Come on Jenny," began Kevin, "We've done our good deed. Let's go!"

"No, I've got an idea," said Jennifer, "OK everybody, let's load the decorations into the sleigh."

As soon as the sleigh was loaded up, Jennifer and Kevin took off again and flew over the giant tree.

"Decorations overboard," shouted Kevin, as streamers, tinsel and lights fell from the sleigh and landed on the tree.

"It's like magic!" cried the villagers excitedly, "Christmas is falling from the sky!"

"Look at those happy people," thought Kevin, and he felt a warm glow inside that had nothing to do with getting presents.

"Coming in for landing!" shouted Santa moments later. "No, don't tell me, we've missed those rascals again!"

"Now that the tree is up," Santa heard one of the villagers saying, "we can go home and wait for our presents."

"Suffering sleighbells!" cried Santa. "Presents! There won't be any presents if I don't catch up with that sleigh."

DWEEEEEE-OH beeped Santa's computer-watch.

"Something's wrong," said Mama Claus at Elf Control. "A big blizzard is jamming our radar and we can't guide you to your sleigh, Santa."

"Well that does it!" groaned Santa as he sat down in Nellie's tiny sleigh. "Now what am I going to do?"

Many miles away, high above the clouds, Kevin and Jennifer were quarrelling.

"If you can't get this sleigh back home," Jennifer said to Kevin, "then I will."

"No, it's MINE!" said Kevin.

"It's not yours," Jennifer clung on tightly.

"I'm in charge," said Kevin, "and I'm going to push THIS button."

WHIRR, WHIRRRRR, WHIRRRRRRRRR!!! The sleigh kicked into overdrive and shot into the night like a comet.

"Hey, how do you stop it?" Kevin cried.

"WHOAAA!!!" shouted Jennifer as the sleigh zoomed off, heading south at top speed.

They pushed buttons and pulled levers, but the sleigh just kept going, with the reindeer, still singing, out in front.

KA-THUMP. They landed in a hot, dusty village, right in the middle of an argument.

"Looks like there's trouble here," said Jennifer, "and we should try to help."

"You stupid donkey, why won't you move?" shouted one man. His donkey was hitched to a cart full of children waiting to celebrate Christmas.

"Don't just sit there, you big dumb ox," shouted the other man whose cart-load of kids was headed the other way. The road was too narrow for both carts to pass. Angry shouts went up.

"Let us pass!" — "No, you back up." — "We were here first!"

Soon, everyone was shouting at the top of their lungs.

Then, as Jennifer and Kevin looked on, an amazing thing happened. The reindeer began to sing a lovely Christmas carol.

"Listen," said Jennifer. "Isn't it beautiful!"

Kevin nodded.

All of a sudden the people stopped arguing and just stood and listened. Then, one by one, they began to join in the singing. Even the animals joined in.

"BRAAAY-A!" sang the donkey.

"BUM DA-DUM!" sang the ox.

"Let's celebrate Christmas right here and now!" said the drivers.

"YAAAY!" shouted all the children.

Jennifer and Kevin joined in the celebration, forgetting all about Santa and his sleigh.

"This is great," said Kevin. "Just singing and celebrating is as much fun as getting presents!"

Jennifer could have said, "I told you so." But she just nodded and smiled.

Santa, Nellie and Elvis were still grounded beside the giant Christmas tree. Santa was frantic.

"How on earth are we going to find the children without any help from Elf Control?" he wondered.

"Don't worry Santa," said Nellie. "Elvis will find them. I told you he has a sixth sense about these things."

"Well, he's done pretty well so far," admitted Santa. "OK Nellie, let's see what your friend can do."

"You hear that, Elvis!" exclaimed Nellie.

"Elvis, ELVIS! Take off your headset and listen for a second! You've got to find Santa's sleigh. Now, go to it kid. You're on!"

Elvis adjusted his antlers, sniffed into the air and took off. Still bopping and snapping, he led the way as they flew into the night.

Back at the village, the cheer of Christmas singing was still in the air.

"That was the best Christmas party ever," said Kevin, as the people started to leave. "I wish it would never end."

"Now we can go home and wait for Santa," said one of the children from the carts.

"Oh, no," shouted Jennifer, "we forgot all about Santa!"

"Come on Jenny," said Kevin, "let's try and get this thing back to him."

"We seem to be on the right course," Kevin said, once they were airborne. Then suddenly the sleigh started drifting down to Earth.

"It's as if it has a mind of its own!" said Kevin, bringing it in to land.

"Where are we?" Jennifer asked as they got out.

The sleigh had landed near a run-down shack. The children stood on tip-toes and peeked through a broken window. What they saw made them very sad.

Inside a bare room sat three children who looked like they were not going to have a very happy Christmas.

"Look at those poor kids," said Kevin. "Jenny, let's help them. Bring me Santa's bag!"

"But it's empty," Jennifer handed him the bag.

"I know the presents are in here somewhere!" Kevin shouted. He shook the bag and pulled it inside out and rightside in, but try as he did to find gifts for the children, the bag remained empty.

Kevin was very angry. Now that he finally understood the spirit of Christmas giving, he couldn't do anything about it.

"That does it," he yelled. "I'm going to get to the bottom of this!" And he opened the bag and jumped right in.

"Kevin, no, wait!" shouted Jennifer.

But it was too late.

"YIKES!" screamed Kevin as he fell and fell. "Doesn't this thing have a bottom?"

CRUNCH. Kevin finally landed. He found himself in a strange world of enormous toys.

"I never should have taken this bag!" he sobbed. "I can't get any of the toys out for those poor kids, I've ruined Christmas by taking Santa's sleigh, and now — I'll never get out of here!"

Suddenly a big gloved hand grabbed Kevin's collar and lifted him up out of the bag.

"Santa," cried Kevin, "boy, am I glad to see you!" He thought for a moment, then said meekly, "I'm sorry Santa, this is all my fault."

"No time for that, young man, I've found you now, thanks to Elvis. Let's leave a roast turkey and some presents for this family and we'll be on our way."

Santa went over to his crew of reindeer.

"They're pooped. I've just begun to deliver the presents and Christmas Eve is almost over."

The gloomy silence was broken by Elvis, who took off his headphones, soft-hoofed over to the sleigh's sound system and plugged in his personal stereo.

Music rang out from the speakers.

"Listen to that!" said Nellie.

"And look at my reindeer!" Santa called out.

One by one, Santa's reindeer began to dip and hop, shuffle and bop, reviving and jiving to the music. Once again the rockin' reindeer had saved the day.

"See, I told you Elvis would come through," said Nellie beaming.

"Well done," said Santa as he gave Elvis a little package, about the size of a tape cassette, from his bag. "You can open this in the morning. Now we all have work to do!"

Kevin took the reins, Jennifer operated the navigation controls and Elvis led the way into the night sky.

Santa started to pull gifts from the bag.

"But how do you do that, Santa?" asked Kevin. "That bag was empty!"

"Ho, Ho, Ho! a little bit of Santa's magic, Kevin," he laughed. "Trade secret."

With Elvis setting the pace and the children piloting, Santa was free to toss gifts out of the back of the sleigh at twice the speed.

"Look out below!" called Santa, as presents fell into houses all over the world.

Christmas was saved!

Santa steered the sleigh back to Kevin and Jennifer's house.

"Come on Elvis, let's get these tired kids home."

The children were already fast asleep when Santa tucked them into their beds.

As the first rays of Christmas morning broke over the horizon, Kevin and Jennifer woke up with a start.

"Jenny," said Kevin scratching his head. "I had this really strange dream."

"So did I," said Jennifer.

"I dreamed that —"

"We flew off in Santa's sleigh and —"

"Wait! Listen!"

From outside came the sound of Christmas carolling.

It was very much like…

"Reindeer singing!" Jennifer and Kevin exclaimed together.

Out into the Christmas dawn the children ran.

"Merry Christmas, Ho, Ho, Ho!"
boomed a deep voice from a long way away...

Also available:

FOLLOW THAT SLEIGH! *VIDEO*

A musical fantasy adventure. Elvis, the rockin' reinder, and a chorus of his doo-wopping friends lead us on a round-the-world chase after Santa's missing sleigh. The video combines vivid clay animation with an original and upbeat musical score based on traditional Christmas melodies.

FOLLOW THAT SLEIGH! *CHRISTMAS ACTIVITY BOOK*

Christmas questions, games, puzzles, information and fun activities for 5 − 10 year olds.

FOLLOW THAT SLEIGH! *ALBUM*

Christmas carols with a whole new twist!
From doo-wop to rap, a zany musical celebration with the cast of *Follow that Sleigh*.

With thanks to:
Bez Ocko, Meg Feeley, Ilana Brody, Anna Immanuel, Tal Zeidani, Sam Orbaum & Carol Corey.